FOR ELOISE,
FROM W. S-F.
R. P.

FOR FRED AND PEGGY, GUIN AND KEITH —
WHO TOOK US UNDER THEIR WINGS
D. P.

First U.S. edition 2009

Library of Congress Cataloging-in-Publication Data is available.

Library of Congress Catalog Card Number 2008935660

ISBN 978-0-7636-3480-3

2 4 6 8 10 9 7 5 3 1

Printed in China

This book was typeset in Truesdell and Herculanum.
The illustrations were done in watercolor and ink.

Candlewick Press
99 Dover Street
Somerville, Massachusetts 02144

visit us at www.candlewick.com

*My mistress
and Lydia*

*My master,
Gaius Martius*

Marcus and Lucullus

Apollo

ROMAN DIARY

THE JOURNAL OF ILIONA OF MYTILINI, WHO WAS CAPTURED BY PIRATES AND SOLD AS A SLAVE IN ROME, AD 107

RICHARD PLATT

illustrated by DAVID PARKINS

CANDLEWICK PRESS

·CONTENTS·

NOTES FOR THE READER ON ILIONA'S WORLD

Cratinus

Cestius

Cytheris

Our doorman

The overseer

A new diary for my new life in Egypt, year 3 of the 221st Olympiad.

My thoughts run faster than my pen as I write this, for today I learned that our lives are about to change — we are to sail to Egypt on a galley that leaves the day after tomorrow!

We must make this sudden journey because my father has learned that a warehouse he owns in Egypt has burned to the ground. He must travel there immediately to see it rebuilt. Mother, my brother, Apollo, and I will all travel with him to make our home in Alexandria for two years at least.

It is a thrilling and wonderful idea, for I have never left our Greek island before. We have a fine, big house here on Mytilini, but in Egypt we will have an even bigger one. Everything else will be different, too. This is why I have begun a diary, so that I might write down all that we do each day and record everything new while it is still fresh.

To help in this project, my mother has given me a writing set: a bundle of fine goose quills tied with a purple ribbon, a knife to sharpen them with, a traveling ink pot, and a roll of the finest papyrus I have ever seen. Its surface is as smooth as the skin on Apollo's back.

In just two days, we shall board our ship in the harbor here and set sail from Mytilini across the warm Aegean Sea. I think I shall like to stand at the front, let down my hair, and feel the salt wind comb and curl it! In little more than a week, we shall be in Alexandria. I cannot wait for this adventure to begin. . . .

ILIONA

DISASTER·STRIKES·US!

FIRST DAY OF OUR VOYAGE

This morning before dawn, we came aboard our ship. As the sun rose, the crew put out their oars and began to beat a splashing tune on the water. From land, I have often watched boats leaving the harbor: they seem to glide gracefully over the blue sea. From the deck, the view is different: a hundred men or more must strain every muscle to push the boat forward.

This morning, though, the crew did not labor for long. The wind blew from the land, and once a sail was raised, they could rest. I stood at the front of the ship with Apollo to let the wind comb my hair, as I had dreamed. Instead it teased it into a knotted mass, which took an hour to untangle!

FIFTH DAY

Pity us! Apollo and I have lost everything we loved and cherished. Now we are orphans and slaves, to be bought and sold like goats.

We were but half a day from Rhodes when a sail appeared behind us. From the shape of the ship and the way it cut through the water, the crew could tell that it was a pirate craft. Our mariners rushed to

 their oars, but though they strained and pulled, the dark outline grew ever bigger behind us.

In the battle that followed, my mother drowned and my father was run through with a pirate sword. My tears flowed, but I could do nothing. The pirates were not interested in the ship's cargo of wine but only in taking slaves, which they called "self-loading cargo." They took from Apollo and me all we possessed except my ink, pens, and papyrus. These they let me keep because they think I will fetch a better price if it is obvious that I know my letters.

Our journey to Egypt is at an end. Now we have begun another journey, to the very center of the world: Rome.

❀❀❀

The pirates quickly sorted us out. They fed the old, ill, and crippled to the fish.

The pirate ship's ram shattered the deck rail.

WE·ARE·SOLD

MY THIRD DAY IN ROME

We reached this strange and enormous city two days ago — not directly, but by hopping like frogs, for we were bought and sold three times on the way.

At each auction, Apollo and I clung to each other, in case we should be sold apart, but — praise be to Zeus — it has not happened. Instead, other children have joined our miserable band. At each auction, our price rises (though mine more than Apollo's, for I can speak fluent Latin and read a few words, but he struggles to write even in Greek). Finally we came into the port of Ostia on a stinking barge, which I think must have carried rotten fish before us.

We were herded quickly through the streets to some dark, cramped lodgings. We had food to eat — bread, oil, and olives — but we were all filthy from our long journey. Creatures moved in my hair; my clothes were like rags, and my eyes were red from crying.

Today two women came to the room in which we were locked with the other children. They took us out and gave us water and oil to wash with. Then they cleaned our hair with fine-toothed combs to remove the lice and gave us new garments to wear. I could not help but enjoy this, until one of my companions snapped, "Idiot! Can't you see that they are preparing us for sale again?"

During the journey to Rome, we traveled on foot (much) . . .

by ship (also much) . . .

in a cart (twice) . . .

and on donkeys (once).

MY FOURTH DAY

The women returned this morning. They hung wooden signs around each of our necks. I was quite pleased that I could read the Latin words on mine: "Greek maiden." They also dusted our feet with chalk. This, I learned, was to show that we were newly taken as slaves, and so likely to be a troublesome buy.

"Greeks for sale!" the traders shouted as they pushed Apollo and me onto a little platform so that everyone in the crowd could see us clearly.

The bidding was brisk, and we were sold to a tall man who bought no other slaves in the sale. As he pressed through the crowd toward us, I was relieved that Apollo and I had been bought as a single lot — but, anxious about what would become of us, I asked the man where we were going. He cocked his head and raised his eyebrows, as if he couldn't have been more surprised to hear a dog speak Latin.

"You're the property of Gaius Martius," he replied. "He's a senator, and I'm his overseer. You'll work in his *domus* here in Rome." He turned Apollo's right hand over to look at the palm. "Judging by the smoothness of his hands," he said, "your brother has never done a stroke of work, but he'll be useful on my master's farm in the hills." Then he pushed us forward into the square. "Come on. Shake that chalk off your feet!"

The trader sang my praises, saying I could read and write. He said rather less about my brother.

I·SAY·FAREWELL·TO·APOLLO

THE SIXTH DAY

My parting from Apollo came sooner than I had dreamed possible, for, seeing me sob all the way from the auction, the overseer clearly decided he'd have no peace until we were separated.

When we reached the house, he pushed me into a little room and bolted the door. I hammered with my fists but simply got bruised and splintered. I lay on the bed and tried to forget I was a prisoner by writing everything that had happened that morning in this journal.

I must have slept afterward, for when I awoke, the door was open and a little lamp burned in an alcove in the wall, casting shadows across the room. When one of them moved, I sat up quickly.

"Don't be afraid," the shadow said, and I saw its owner, a girl a couple of years older than me. She told me she was a slave too and that I would be happy here, for the master was a kind and generous man. "And his wife doesn't whip us unless we deserve it!" she added. I asked her name, but before answering, she leaned out of the door and bellowed, "She is awake!"

She had just told me she was called Cytheris when a tall and finely dressed woman swept into the room and shooed her out.

"Iliona — that is your name, isn't it?" the woman asked, turning to me. "I want you to know how welcome you are," she said, but didn't smile.

*Apollo and I wept bitterly
when the overseer separated us.*

I asked if I could see Apollo. She looked puzzled, then left the room. A moment later, my little brother shuffled in.

I jumped up and threw my arms around his neck. We sat for a moment on the bed together, but before we had time to say much, the woman came back. In her arms was a sleeping child, about a year old.

The overseer followed her in, so I guessed what was to come. I screamed and begged him not to take Apollo, but it made no difference. He pushed us roughly apart.

Seeing my tears, the woman sat down and put her arm around my shoulder. This started me sobbing again, and the child awoke. I thought she would cry too, but instead she grabbed my hand and began sucking on my little finger.

More gently this time, her mother — my new mistress — began talking to me again. I was to be a companion and teacher for little Lydia, she said. I would also teach Greek to Lydia's half brothers, Marcus and Lucullus. "We wanted to buy you because you already knew some Latin," she explained.

Her arm around my shoulder, the warmth of the room, the child in her arms — all these things reminded me of home and my own mother — not in a sad way but (to my surprise) in a way that comforted me. And for a moment I forgot my sorrow and began to wonder if I might be happy here.

Apollo's hands were untied now,
so he could hug me.

MY·STUDIES·BEGIN·AGAIN

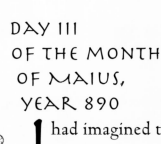

DAY III OF THE MONTH OF MAIUS, YEAR 890

I had imagined that a slave's life here in Rome would be one of locks and chains, but there is nothing like that to keep me from running away.

Yet where would I run to, and why would I try? I am beginning to see that in Rome, slavery and freedom are not opposites, like night and day or winter and summer. The poorest Roman citizens are worse off than many slaves. Here I have clothes (though it's true they are simple linen), my stomach never aches with hunger (though the food is plain), and I can rest when I am tired.

It would be simple to distract the doorman and slip into the street.

I sleep in a room with Cytheris, and in this I feel I am lucky. She keeps me company and is teaching me much about Rome. Last night I learned about the calendar. Romans count the years from the date Rome was founded. The months are about thirty days long and are each differently named. The days are more difficult, and for now I will just make my diary by counting up from the first day of each month.

DAY IV

This day I began my studies. It was also the first time I had set foot outside since the auction. I had expected to study at home, as girls always do in Greece. But instead I went to school with Marcus and Lucullus. The three of us walked there through the streets with Cestius, the boys' *pedagogus*.

Cestius is an old slave: part tutor, part guardian.

The boys tormented a flea-bitten dog.

I was surprised at how humble the school is. On Mytilini, Apollo studied in a grand building with a hundred other boys. This one was just a tiny room with a few stools and an armchair for the teacher. Cestius made fun of my surprise: "This is one of the better ones!" he told me. "Most boys sit in the street to study."

Our class was not so different from my brother's school in Mytilini. Mostly we write on the same wax-coated tablets, though my *stylus* is shaped like the letter *T*. With its flat end I can smooth out the wax when I make mistakes, which I think is a fine idea, for I make many.

We studied reading and writing from early morning until noon, when Cestius came back. We walked home along Etruscan Street, which is lined with the most exotic kinds of shops.

In fact, my nose found the street before my eyes did, because all the incense and perfume sellers have their stalls here.

The street is very busy, and Cestius took my hand. "Keep your eyes peeled," he told us, "for there are thieves around every corner here. They will skin you alive and sell you back your own hide before you even realize you've been robbed."

We saw no thieves, but we did have to flatten ourselves against the wall as a huge cart rumbled past, carrying building stone and timber. Our limbs seemed to be more at risk than our purses!

The cart had solid wooden wheels and was pulled by a grumpy ox.

WE·VISIT·NERO'S·BATHS

DAY XVI OF MAIUS ✿

Tomorrow we shall visit the baths. Though we have a bathroom here, with a small tub, Cytheris tells me we are going somewhere altogether more grand — to the baths of Nero, who ruled Rome fifty years ago. Cytheris says he was a cruel man hated by all Romans. His reputation earned him a saying: "What could be worse than Nero, or better than his baths?"

❀❀❀

DAY XVII

How can I begin to describe Nero's baths? They are more like a palace. The huge building towers above the neighborhood; a gurgling "aqueduct" (a river on legs) brings water from the distant hills, and steam pours from the windows. The baths are so cheap they are almost free. Anyone who has a *quadrans* — Rome's smallest coin — can soak all afternoon.

It seemed that a visit to the baths was a chance for my mistress to show off how many slaves she can afford, for she insisted that every one of us come with her. We set off in the afternoon: two carried her in a litter, one walked ahead, and the rest of us followed.

Once we were inside and had changed into our *subligari* and *mamillares*, my mistress set one of us to guard our clothes and took two more to wash, oil, and massage her. The rest of us could do as we pleased for the afternoon.

Cytheris took me from room to room until we came to the hot bath, the steamy *caldarium*. Here we lounged, pampering each other until we met some friends of Cytheris's. When she introduced me as newly enslaved, they were all very sorry for me.

As we talked, each revealed how she had become a slave. Most had been born of slave parents, but one blond girl, from Germany, had been taken by Roman soldiers when they crushed a revolt there.

❀❀❀

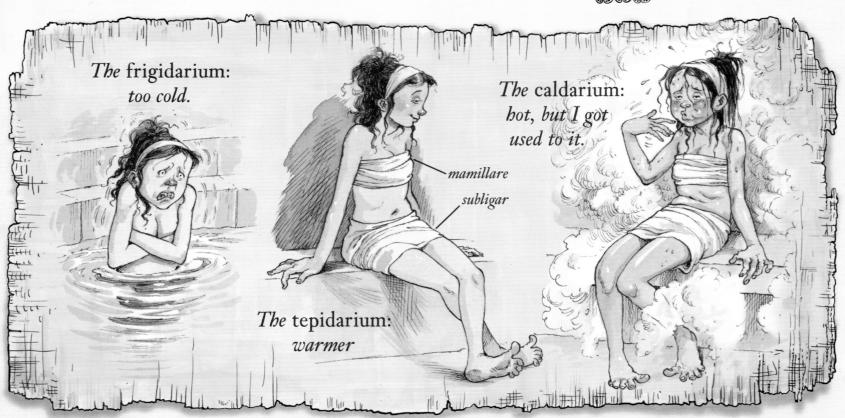

The frigidarium: *too cold.*

The tepidarium: *warmer*

mamillare

subligar

The caldarium: *hot, but I got used to it.*

Cytheris showed me how to use a strigil *to scrape my skin and rubbed me with perfumed oil, which I guess she had drained from our mistress's bottle while her back was turned.*

DAY XX

A fortnight ago, I wrote a letter to Apollo and gave it to my mistress. She promised that the overseer, who regularly travels between Rome and the farm, would take it to him, but I have had no reply.

DAY XXV

This morning I awoke with a thundercloud around my head. I had dreamed that Apollo and I were back on Mytilini, doing the things we used to do together before we were captured — running on the open hills and swimming in the sea. When I awoke, the walls around me felt like a prison.

My master saw my long face, and I told him about my dream. He tried to make me feel better about living here in Rome, finishing by saying, "There is always a chance of manumission." I didn't understand this Latin word, so he explained that good and obedient slaves may be freed through the kindness of their masters or may buy their freedom with the money they earn.

His words lifted my stifling gloom, and I began to hope that I might not live my whole life as a slave.

It's the noise of the baths that you notice first: an echoing clamor as (it seems) half the population of Rome has come to bathe.

I·AM·SENT·ON·AN·ERRAND

DAY XXVII OF MAIUS

I learned today that the older brother of Marcus and Lucullus is a legionnaire who soon will be returning to Rome for the triumph of the emperor Trajan. This grand parade is to celebrate the victory of Roman forces in Dacia, and it will be a fantastic spectacle that all of Rome will watch.

❁❁❁

DAY XXIX

I made the mistake of talking to Cytheris about manumission. "Are you mad?" she exploded. "We earn a few *asses*' pocket money a week for our sweat and toil around this house. There are 16 *asses* in a *denarius*. They paid 500 *denarii* for you. It would take three lifetimes of work for you to buy your freedom." Then she threw a cushion at me and ran from the room in tears.

Now I am as full of sorrow as before — and guilt, too, for having reminded her of how hopelessly trapped we both are.

❁❁❁

"Do the arithmetic, Iliona!" Cytheris yelled.

"The dogs and bedbugs left last night, and when they go, only a madman stays!" the seamstress muttered.

DAY I OF THE MONTH OF IUNIUS

My mistress sent me on an errand this morning. It was the first time I have ventured out into Rome's streets on my own. My task was to collect some embroidery from a seamstress who lived on the top floor of an apartment block.

Even by the standards of Rome, which are low, the building was a crumbling wreck. The seamstress was hurrying to pack and practically threw the work at me. "The walls will come down, Greek girl," she warned me, "sure as Trajan's the emperor."

As I hurried down the stairs, I saw everyone else who dwelled or worked there leaving. One just jerked his thumb over his shoulder and said, "Hasten!" A huge crack had appeared in the side of the building! I did just that and breathed a sigh of relief when I was out in the street once more.

But my ordeal was not yet over. It was no great distance back to my home, but the streets lack signs and names, and finding your way is more like guesswork than navigation. In my haste, I took a wrong turn and in vain gazed about me for a shop, a house, a tree that I recognized. As I struggled, I heard a voice behind me.

"Are you lost?"

I spun around to face an elderly, white-haired man dressed in a clean and neatly pressed toga. Such was my panic that I could not remember a word of Latin and answered in Greek. "Yes! Where am I?"

To my amazement, he replied in Greek. "I am Greek too, though I have lived here most of my life. Where do you live?"

I told him that my master's house was on the Quirinal Hill, not far from Hill Gate and close to where a huge fig tree grows. "I know the place," the old man said. He beckoned to me to follow, and within a fourth part of an hour, he had led me home.

I turned around to thank my new-found friend, but he was already ten paces away. "You are lucky. Gaius Martius is a good man," he called over his shoulder.

I was too far away to reply, so I just waved. I wonder if I will see him again to thank him properly for his help?

I never expected to meet another Greek so soon.

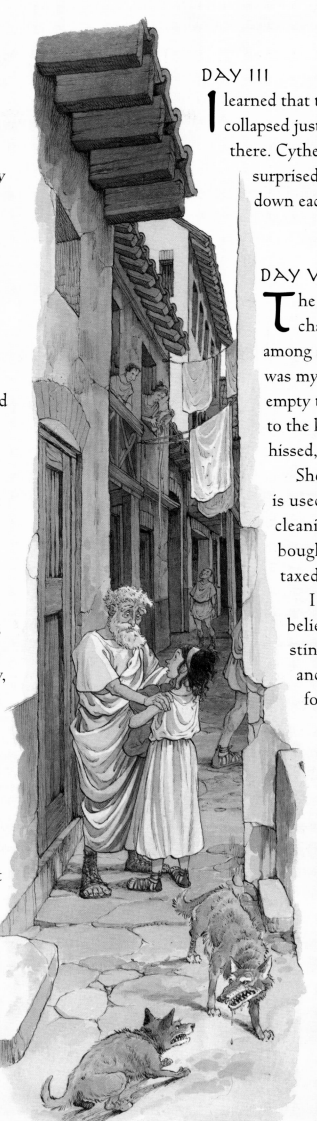

DAY III

I learned that the apartments I visited collapsed just an hour after I was there. Cytheris didn't even seem surprised. "Two or three come down each week," she said.

DAY V

The task of emptying the chamber pots is shared among all the slaves. Today it was my turn. I was about to empty them into the drain next to the kitchen when Cytheris hissed, "Stop!"

She explained that urine is used here in Rome for cleaning clothes and is bought and sold and even taxed!

I found this hard to believe, but that night a stinking wagon drew up and the driver tipped the foul liquid into a jar.

For this (Cytheris told me), we receive a few *quadrantes* each week. I have decided that I shall save mine to buy Apollo's freedom.

I·MEET·A·SOLDIER

DAY VII OF IUNIUS

We were woken last night by a tremendous tumult. My master's eldest son, Cratinus, had returned. He had tried to slip in through the back door without attracting attention, but instead awoke the doorman, who took him for an intruder and challenged him. By the time the misunderstanding had been untangled, the whole house was awake and gathered in the *peristylum*.

Cratinus seemed to me very haughty and pleased with himself, and I was soon bored with the spectacle and slipped back to bed.

DAY VIII

Cratinus is just like the soldiers who guard the fort on Mytilini: they think armor and scars make it impossible for girls to resist their charms. I had to endure an hour of his stories about how brave he had been in Dacia. It was dull in the extreme, though he did make me laugh once or twice.

DAY X

I foolishly smiled at Cratinus this morning when I was in the kitchen preparing food for baby Lydia. Taking this as encouragement, he pinched my bottom. I spun around and spat out my fury at him, ending with, "And if you pinch me again, I shall tell your parents!"

At this, he threw back his head and laughed. "Tell them. Tell anyone you like. Tell all of Rome. For you are just a slave girl, and I can do whatever I like."

I think he would have gone further if I had not been holding a kitchen knife. But he just picked up a fig, pushed it whole into his fat mouth, and walked out into the *atrium*.

DAY XI

Cratinus has injured his foot. He was showing off to his brothers in the *peristylum*, pretending to assault a statue, when his sword glanced off its marble arm and nearly took off one of his toes. Now he worries that he will not be able to march in Emperor Trajan's triumph in four days' time. I shall be glad if he cannot.

A burglar the size of Cratinus could not really be stopped by our elderly doorman.

DAY XIII

At dinner today, I brought in a dish just as the family were teasing Cratinus about his endless war stories. Suddenly he lost his temper. "Do you want to know what Dacia was really like?" he yelled. Without waiting for a reply, he continued: "Shall I tell you how Decebalus set fire to everything as he retreated so that we would have nothing to eat as we followed him?

"Or perhaps you'd like to know about the Battle of Tapae? Oh, yes, our emperor's great victory — but it wasn't quite as glorious as you may have heard. The grass was red with Roman blood, and there were so many injured that

the emperor tore his cloak into strips to make bandages."

For a moment, it was so quiet that I could hear the fountain outside in the *atrium*, then our master said quietly, "Cratinus, we know how much you have suffered, but there are children here. Why don't you go and rest?"

Cratinus got up and slowly left the room.

After that, I felt a little sorry for Cratinus. All the same, I was relieved to learn from Cytheris that he will not be with us for much longer. His legion will leave Rome directly after the triumph.

✿✿✿

Cratinus's smile, which has hardly left his face since he arrived, vanished.

Soldiers struck victorious poses on the huge floats.

WE·WATCH·THE·TRIUMPH!

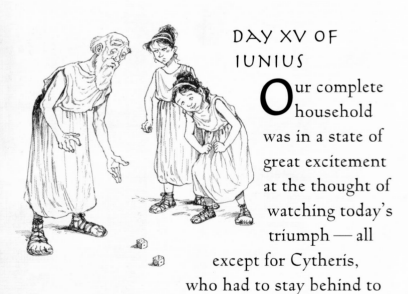

DAY XV OF IUNIUS

Our complete household was in a state of great excitement at the thought of watching today's triumph — all except for Cytheris, who had to stay behind to look after little Lydia. We had been fighting for a week over which of us would go. In the end Cestius tossed dice and I won, which threw Cytheris into a great sulk.

It was still dark when we left the house, but the streets were turned almost as bright as day by the torches of the people who had flocked to see the spectacle. They so crowded

the street that my master and mistress were forced to abandon their sedan chairs and walk like common people. They shuffled slowly to Octavian's Walks, where the senators and other dignitaries were to greet the emperor. I went with Marcus, Lucullus, Cestius, and the other seven slaves to find a place to stand.

We seemed to wait forever before there was anything to look at. While we hopped impatiently from foot to foot, I spotted some distance away the white-haired Greek who had helped me home. I yelled and waved, but he did not hear me. Then a terrific roar from the crowd told us the parade had begun, and a moment later soldiers in brilliant, shiny armor filled the road to the bursting point.

I looked for Cratinus, thinking I would spot him from his limp, but all the troops marched in perfect time. Then I saw the emperor himself, in a magnificent golden chariot, drawn by four white horses. A slave held a laurel wreath above his head. He wore no helmet, and I realized for the first time that he was just a man like any other.

When I told Cestius I thought I had expected to see a god, he snorted. "All emperors think they're gods."

When Trajan and more of his troops had passed, I picked up my cloak. But Marcus hissed, "Not YET! WATCH!" Turning back, I thought I was seeing something magical. For around the corner came an entire building, several stories in height. A hundred bearers carried it on their shoulders, moving at a brisk walk. Another of these great floats followed, then many more, so that the procession continued for another hour.

Following behind was a sad sight: thousands of chained prisoners taken captive in the war with the Dacians walked behind their leaders. These men all knew they were living their last minutes.

The crowd now began to press toward the Forum to see the fate that awaits those who oppose the mighty Roman Empire. But I had no taste for this, and even the boys looked pale.

We hurried home as quickly as we could.

Centurions led the defeated leaders to the Forum.

The job of the slave holding the wreath is to whisper in the emperor's ear, "Remember that you're only human," right through the parade.

I·VISIT·THE·SENATE

DAY XX OF IUNIUS

I am soon to see my brother again! As I sat with Lydia this afternoon, Cytheris came and told me that in one month we shall be traveling to my master's estate in the Sabine Hills. We shall stay there through the hottest weeks of the summer — and I shall have the chance to spend some time with Apollo, if his work allows. I am glad, for he has not replied to any of the letters I have sent him.

DAY XXII

This day our master went to sit in the Senate, which always causes much upheaval. He dreads going but loves it when he gets there. Making Rome's laws makes him feel important, and he sees all his friends. Most are very old, and I suspect that they take secret bets on which of them will die first.

It was halfway through the morning when my mistress let out a shriek. "Hell's teeth, he's left his medicine behind!" I looked around, and sure enough, in a niche by the door was my master's flask of sea-grape wine. "Iliona, take it to him, or truly he will cough his lungs up."

I dashed to the Forum and rushed through the door of the Senate House without stopping. Too late, I realized that the passageway led straight into the Senate chamber. I found myself surrounded by Rome's greatest, richest men.

The room fell silent.

"Young lady," a senator finally addressed me, "I assume that your dramatic appearance is of the utmost importance, since the very future of Rome hangs upon the debate it interrupted."

Scanning the rows of seats, I spotted my master and held up the flask. "Senator Martius, you forgot your sea-grape wine."

There was another unbearable silence. Then I heard a stifled snigger from a younger senator at the back. One of his neighbors guffawed, and at length laughter echoed around the chamber. When it died down, someone shouted, "Take your potion, Gaius. Your coughing has been been driving us all mad!"

As the laughter started again, a hand pulled the vial from my grip, and it was passed back to my master.

I didn't wait to see him drink, but fled the chamber as quickly as I had entered it.

In the Senate, my master wears a purple-edged toga and special red shoes with a crescent stitched to the front.

OUR·WATER·DRIES·UP

This morning there was silence from the kitchen, which normally rings with the sound of water flowing endlessly from a pipe on the wall into a stone basin below.

"The aqueduct has burst once more!" my mistress exclaimed when she came down.

In Mytilini, water always came from a well, never from a spout in the wall. She explained that our water here comes from springs four days' journey away. "It's beautiful, clear water, but to flow here, it crosses deep valleys on high, arched bridges. In other places it flows underground, through tunnels. Because of its length — more than 60,000 paces — the channel is always leaking."

In my first week in Rome, I had marveled at the luxury of having water running in the house but soon took it for granted. Now I appreciate it once more, for I have to pick up an *amphora* and join a long line of slaves at the fountain in the street outside.

The slaves from the houses nearby have a rare chance to talk together at the fountain.

DAY II

Little Lydia said her first Greek word today! It was *Mamme* — Mom in Greek. I cannot tell my mistress. She would be furious if she knew I spoke Greek to the baby and madder still if she knew Lydia thought I was her mother!

❀❀❀

DAY V

We still have no water in the house, and today an errand took me past the aqueduct. From a gap in its side spills a torrent of water that rushes down onto the roofs of the houses below. On the bridge I saw stonemasons at work trying to block the hole with bags full of sand. Quite a crowd had gathered to watch, and I listened as a man shouted angrily at the supervisor of the water repairs. Judging from his fine new toga, he was very wealthy.

"Why do the street fountains still flow when the water in my house has dried up?" the rich man demanded. "Beggars may drink, while my fountain is silent!"

The supervisor of the water repairs let out a deep sigh before replying with exaggerated respect: "Because, sir, inside the *castellum* there is a barrier. Normally there is enough water to flow over it and into the pipes that lead into your fine abode"— here he made a little bow —"but if the aqueduct bursts or leaks, the level falls. Then your pipes are cut off, but water continues to flow to the public fountains. In this way"— he paused before delivering his crushing last line —"the poorest

The rich man's sandals got soaked as he listened to the explanation.

citizens in Rome do not have the free water taken from them by those who can afford a supply to their own homes."

This bold response brought a round of applause, for we had all expected the official to grovel to such a wealthy, important man.

Sniffing defeat, the man edged away, muttering, "Ah, yes, I see. Thank you for that clear explanation," as he tried to hide his embarrassment.

❀❀❀

I returned past Cloaca Maxima, the city's biggest sewer, which stank in the summer heat.

WE·SET·OFF·FOR·THE·FARM

DAY XX OF IULIUS

We were supposed to leave for the country today, but during a thunderstorm last night, lightning bolts flashed in the direction of the Sabine Hills and everyone (but me) feared it was a sign that we should not travel.

To check whether it was truly a bad omen, my mistress went to the temple of Jupiter Tonans, a thunder god, taking with her an offering of a chicken. (Cytheris says she cannot think the omen too serious, or she would have taken a pig at least.) She came back saying that it is safe to travel, so we depart tomorrow.

DAY XI

On this day I was woken by the snorts and braying of the donkeys and the iron-ringed wheels of the two *raedae* they were pulling. We were to make an early start, since builders' carts are the only wagons allowed into the crowded streets during the day.

"Get a move on!" the driver was grumbling when I went outside. "I'll be fined if we're not through Hill Gate by dawn."

I helped the others load the carriages with everything we would need on our journey. (Fortunately we had little luggage: most of it had left yesterday on a train of mules.) Then we flung ourselves inside.

And so we set off, driving along High Lane in complete darkness, guided by torches on the front-most carriage.

By the time the sun rose, we had left the walls of Rome behind us and were traveling through fields of waving flowers. These made me long for Mytilini, for in spring the hills there are a mass of different colors. These flowers, though, were in rows and all alike, and Cestius tells me they are grown for the vases of the city. In other fields lettuce and vegetables grew, and huge flocks of chickens scratched in the dust.

The heat, the early start, the rocking of the carriage, and the unchanging view (for the road was dead straight) all competed to see which could make me drowsy first.

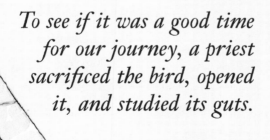

To see if it was a good time for our journey, a priest sacrificed the bird, opened it, and studied its guts.

Cytheris told me the postman might travel 100 miles in a day — three times as far as our creaking raeda *would carry us.*

My head flopped, and I jerked it upright a dozen times before finally falling fast asleep. A loud shout woke me, and Cytheris grabbed my arm. I had slumped sideways and was about to fall out of the carriage tailgate.

I was shaking like a reed in a gale when she pulled me back inside. The road is surfaced with square stones so that it can resist the heaviest wagons without breaking up. Worse, the shout had come from a postman riding his horse at a gallop. Between the hard road and his horse's hooves, my head would have been well and truly broken had I fallen.

When at last we arrived at the farm, it was dark once more. Marcus and Lucullus leaped down at the end of the drive and raced ahead of us to the door, which was lit by torches. More of these cast puddles of light on a few patches of white wall and overhanging olive trees. Everything else disappeared into inky darkness.

Before we left Rome, I had imagined that I would rush around the farm until I found Apollo, but I was so exhausted that I simply collapsed onto my bed and fell instantly asleep.

❀❀❀

My master's villa in the Sabine Hills is very grand.

I·FIND·MY·BROTHER!

DAY XXII OF IULIUS

From the moment I awoke this morning, I could think only of finding Apollo. Yet this was the very thing I could not do, for the villa is a very different place from our house in Rome. There, my master and mistress lead busy lives and hardly notice if one of us is missing. Here, they are idle, with nothing better to do than to count us and ask, "Where's Cytheris?" or "I haven't seen Iliona for some time. Where's she gone?"

So instead of searching for my brother, I had to be content with glancing from the windows to see if I could spot him. When I finally plucked up the courage to ask whether I could see Apollo, my mistress said curtly, "Perhaps tomorrow," and sent me to put the baby to bed.

Here Cytheris and I have separate rooms. We all retired early to bed this evening, which has given me plenty of time to write in this diary.

✿✿✿

DAY XXV

I have finally met Apollo! Having seen me sulking and kicking my heels about my tasks, my master asked me what the matter was, and I said I longed to see my brother.

"Then you shall!" he said, and sent a message that the bailiff, who runs the farm, should fetch him.

32

*I hardly recognized Apollo —
his hair was matted and greasy,
and he stank like a goat.*

When the bailiff finally arrived with a boy, I stared and blinked. Was this Apollo? Only when he spoke my name was I sure, and I ran and threw my arms around him. Then I stood back and gazed at him. He was quite changed. He wasn't just thinner; he had bruises on his arms and a red scar around one ankle. Worse, perhaps, were his eyes. They darted left and right, and he had the expression that I once saw on the face of a stag as it fled from the hunt.

I asked him if he was all right, and before answering, Apollo turned to the bailiff. Only when the man nodded did he reply — and then in stuttering Latin. "I'm fine," he said. "They treat us well here. The work is not too hard, and we get enough to eat. . . ."

All this came without expression, like the worst actors I had seen in the theater on Mytilini. Then he said in Greek, "I've missed you, but I cannot stay long. We are weeding the vines, and if I don't return, my friends will have to do my row as well as their own. Good-bye."

He kissed me and was gone.

❁❁❁

DAY XXVI

I have made friends with the house dogs. They are huge and black — whereas the herders' dogs are all white. I was curious about this and asked the bailiff, who told me, "Why, think about it, girl. A guard dog must be black so that thieves who come in the night cannot see him. A herder's dog is better off white so that he is not mistaken for a wolf."

*The house dogs scared
me at first.*

SECRETS·OF·THE·FARM

DAY XXVII OF IULIUS

Last night I was woken by the small noise of something dry and hard falling on the floor of my room.

Outside, I heard the slap of bare feet running from my window. I crawled around to try to find whatever had been thrown in, but it was too dark. In the morning, I found a short piece of bone. One side was scratched in a pattern. I took it to the window, and in the sunlight, I realized I was holding it upside down.

There, in tiny Greek letters, was a message: COME OUR HUTS IN 2 NIGHTS.

I didn't know how Apollo found out which room was mine. Nor did I think I could wait that long to see him again, but I had no choice. So I continued with my tasks as if I were still in Rome.

Here, though, time seems to crawl past, for in fact, there is little for us to do. This morning my mistress decided that she would like to take a walk with the baby while Cestius was teaching the boys. What this really meant was that she walked while I carried Lydia.

From the road we could look down at row upon row of vines stretching down into the valley — and up, to the steeper slopes lined with olive trees. My mistress's conversation was mostly about how difficult it was to make money from a vineyard. I paid little attention until I heard her saying, "And that's where the laborers live."

❀❀❀

My mistress pointed down the hill to a row of low shacks.

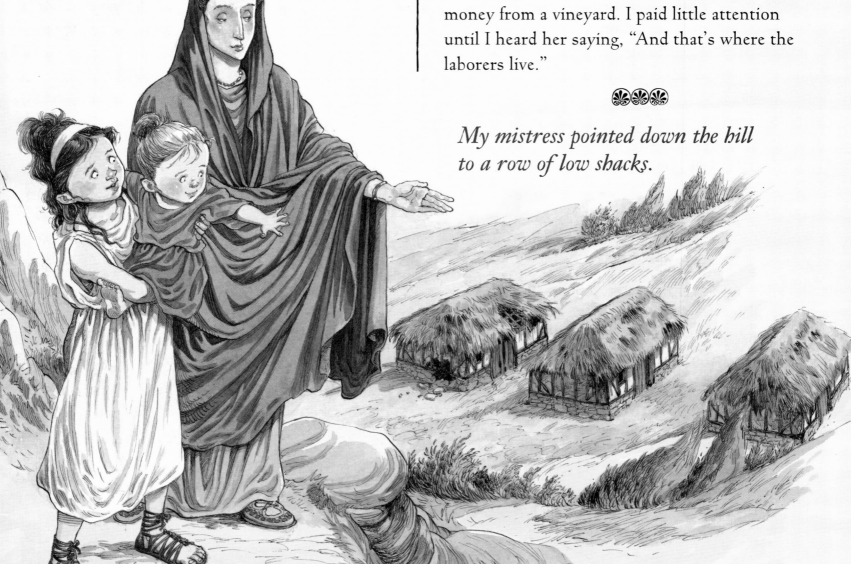

Apollo lifted his shirt to show me his flat stomach. "I am often hungry," he said.

DAY XXIX

Zeus must have been smiling on me last night, for there was a full moon. Once everyone was in bed, I had no difficulty slipping out the window and running down the drive through the moon shadows of the olive trees. Now I have learned the truth about Apollo's life on the farm.

"Iliona, I can't begin to describe how awful it is here," he told me. "We are prisoners. We live mostly on coarse bread and olives and work eight days in every nine from dawn until dusk."

I asked him what happened to his ankle.

"One of us tried to escape. They picked him up, whipped him, shaved his head, and branded his leg with an *F* for *fugitivus*—a runaway."

"But your ankle?"

"I'm coming to that. The overseer said we must all have known about the escape, so for a month we worked in chains. Then Gaius Martius arrived without warning one day and saw what we were enduring. He fired the overseer and put an old slave in his place. Now things are not as bad as they were—we have new clothes and time to rest in the hottest hours."

A dog began to bark, and I was glad I had made friends with them. Apollo poked his head out of the hut. "You had better go. Don't try to come here again. It will be trouble for both of us." He pushed me out, and I sprinted back to the villa.

Only this morning did I realize how close I had come to discovery, for the daylight revealed my dusty footprints, leading from the drive to my window!

FIRE!

DAY XV OF THE MONTH OF AUGUSTUS

Our stay in the hills finished yesterday, and we are back in Rome. I did not see Apollo again, apart from when we came only close enough to wave. My mistress frowned a silent warning when I asked if we could talk.

We had one exciting moment when rumors spread of slaves deserting a nearby farm. The shutters went up, and the dogs were released in case we should all have our throats cut in the night by the *fugitivi*. In the end, though, it turned out to be false gossip.

DAY XX

Yesterday I nearly lost my life — and became a heroine (though I am not sure I deserve the glory heaped on my shoulders)!

The day began normally enough: we set out for Agrippa's baths (not as nice as Nero's, for the water is less clear). We did not linger as long as usual, but instead went to the house of my mistress's friend nearby. Lydia was sleeping, and I took her crib to the other end of the house.

Not long after, there was a smell of smoke. Nobody was concerned, for there is always smoke in Rome from people lighting cooking or heating fires with small wood, to set the charcoal alight. But the conversation turned to fires, such as the great fire fifty years ago that destroyed most of Rome.

Even when we heard cries in the street, there was no alarm. Our hostess looked out but returned, saying, "The fire is distant, and the wind blows it away from here."

But then came a loud hammering at the door. A boy hardly older than me, his face black with soot, asked for buckets, adding, "Look out! The flames are attacking your walls!" At this exact moment, a billow of smoke blew into the room, as if Adranos, the fire god himself, had heard him.

Everyone rushed toward the *peristylum*. As soon as we got outside, we heard loud crackling and felt heat on our faces. Hungry flames licked toward the room where Lydia slept, but nobody did anything. While my mistress sobbed, all the other women wrung their hands. One muttered, "At least it isn't a male child."

Their stupidity made me furious and foolhardy. I plunged into the pool in the middle of the *peristylum* to soak my clothes and covered my face with my wet scarf. Then I dashed toward the open door.

For the rest of my story, I rely on others, for all I remember is waking up in bed at home and immediately retching a foul black paste onto the bedclothes. When the room ceased to spin around me, I saw Cytheris, who whispered, "I fetched our master from the Senate," and pointed to where he stood with my mistress at the end of the bed. They beamed, and my mistress said quietly, "You did a brave and fine thing, Iliona. We shall not forget this."

It seems that I stumbled from the smoke and flames, dropped the crib and its squealing passenger, and fainted.

I·LIVE·AT·THE·WORLD'S·CENTER

DAY XXV OF AUGUSTUS

Today my mistress received a letter from her brother, a legionary commander stationed on the outer edges of the empire. He is on a big cold island called Britannia, somewhere far to the north. It is farther even than Dacia, where Cratinus fought. And he does not like it.

The letter started an argument between my master and mistress. When she took her brother's part — that Britannia is cold and the people ignorant and not worth ruling — my master shrugged. "You forget, my dear, that Rome grows strong by conquest.

From these new provinces we get slaves and treasure. It's true that Britannia is, so far, a disappointment, but from Dacia, Trajan brought back half a million pounds of gold and double that weight of silver. And if the emperor had not defeated the Dacians, they would grow bolder. Soon they would be attacking Rome itself."

❀❀❀

DAY XXVII

On the way to school, I asked Cestius about Rome's provinces, and before our class started, he pointed to a map pinned on the wall. "Look, here is the known world — Rome rules the part colored red. How much is left?" I had to admit that most of the map was red.

When Cestius returned, he led us a different way home, through the Forum. When we reached a food stall, he pointed to everything on sale, saying, "Look: the grain comes from Egypt, the oil from Spain, the salt pork from Gaul — all Roman provinces." Next door, at a hide and fabric shop, the same: "Here is Egyptian linen, African cotton, leather from Britannia, and furs from Asia Minor."

Then he stepped into the street and ran his hand over the shiny

My mistress's brother says that in Britannia sometimes the troops are so cold, they beat their legs with stinging nettles to keep warm.

stone pillar. "The marble that made this pillar came from your country, Iliona. So you see, almost everything we have in Rome comes from distant regions that our great city rules."

DAY XXX

Though my mistress always looks well put together, I had no idea until today how much effort is needed to achieve this effect.

After waiting an hour for Psecas, her *ornatrix*, who comes to the house each day to do her hair, she called me into her room. She was staring into a bronze mirror and applying the finishing touches to her face. She was wearing only an undershirt and called out, "Pass me that clean tunic, Iliona," without taking her eyes away from the mirror. Lying across the bed was a plain white tunic made of the finest silk I have ever seen. I couldn't resist running my hands through the fabric as I handed it to her.

However, it wasn't her clothing that took the time, but her hair. At first she was patient, but when my work collapsed in a clumsy heap around her shoulders, she flew into a rage, shouting words I have only heard women in the marketplace use.

But at last she calmed down, and between us, we made of her hair something that approached its normal appearance. As I left, she gave me four shiny *denarii*, saying, "We shall make an *ornatrix* of you yet, and I can fire that lazy slug Psecas."

I have put the coins under the loose tile on the floor with the others I have been saving to free Apollo.

When I had combed her hair out . . .

I had to primp and pin it . . .

into a neat pile on the top of her head.

WE·WATCH·A·DEADLY·GAME

DAY 11 OF THE MONTH OF SEPTEMBER

I do not know how I should write about what I have seen today. We went to the *munera* — the "games" — at the amphitheater. But these are not like games I have ever played: they are real battles between two slaves, called gladiators, who fight with razor-sharp weapons. Today's games were the gift of the emperor to the people, as part of the celebration of the Dacian tiumph.

The gladiators fight in a big open oval of sand in the middle of the arena. All around rise thousands of seats. To sit in one, you must have a wooden token. My mistress gave one each to Cytheris and me as a treat. "Come and sit with me. We'll be right at the top!"

She wasn't joking. Women and slaves sit on the highest tier, and low seats are reserved for the most important Romans, with senators — such as my master — at the very front. At first I was disappointed to be so far away, but when the spectacle began, I was glad. We could not smell the blood, nor see the fear on the faces of the defeated gladiators.

The first match was between a net man and a pursuer. Though the pursuer fought bravely, he soon grew exhausted. When at last he stumbled, the net man stood with his trident touching the pursuer's chest and turned to the emperor's box for a signal.

I watched this hoplomachus defeat his foe with a well-timed blow from his heavy shield.

The Thracian's shield was so small that he really needed his leg armor.

The net man seemed almost defenseless without a helmet or a sword.

The pursuer's helmet had a rounded crest to keep it from snagging in the net.

The trainer told us that the animals will fight only if they are driven by flaming torches.

I looked away, but my mistress pulled at my arm, saying, "Iliona, don't worry. The pursuer fought well. The emperor will listen to the crowd." Looking up, I saw the emperor spare the defeated man and reward the winner with a wooden sword, which meant he had won his freedom.

During the next fight, I watched everything. And by the third, I was actually enjoying it. The roar of the crowd ringing in my ears swept me along, as a strong wind blows down the road. But when the show ended, I felt ashamed.

As we lined up to get out, we met my master, who had a surprise for us. He led us away from the crowd and down into a basement below the arena. Here we saw ferocious lions, tigers, and leopards pacing in their cages. They will fight in the ring tomorrow afternoon.

The trainer of beasts told us that the animals are usually terrified of the gladiators who challenge them. Despite the excitement of the spectacle, I went home with a sad heart.

The net man was strong and swift and had a determined, scowling face. The citizens below me bet money that he would defeat the pursuer.

Thousands of men swarmed all over the building, just like maggots on a dead dog.

I·AM·HOISTED·INTO·THE·SKY

DAY X OF SEPTEMBER

Today we accompanied my master on a visit to the site of some new baths. People say they will be finer than Nero's — and the biggest that Rome has ever seen. My master is one of the senators who encouraged the emperor to build these baths, in spite of the great cost of their construction.

We left at an early hour, before the sun got too hot. Several of the house slaves carried my master and mistress in chairs. Cytheris and I followed behind, talking. The baths stand just up the hill from the amphitheater, and it is easy to see them from wherever you are in the city.

As we arrived, an important-looking man asked me in Greek, "Would you like to climb to the top?" He must have heard my accent. Of course I replied "Yes!" in Greek, and he called over a mason, who led me to a huge basket.

As soon as I stepped into it, the mason jumped in after me and waved his arm. At this signal, two men began to walk inside a great wheel high above, setting it turning. To my great alarm, this made the basket rise into the air.

Higher and higher it climbed, until I could see every part of the baths. And I was astonished to learn that the walls are but a TRICK! From the outside, they look like solid marble, but in fact, they are not at all.

The mason showed me how the builders mix lime with water and a kind of dust called *pozzolana* so that it turns into a dark gray mess, which they pour between molds made of wooden planks. Within days, the mess turns hard, so that it stands up on its own, without the wooden molds. Then the mason covers it in thin slabs of stone, though they look like solid blocks.

When I got back down to the steady ground, I could not find the Greek man to thank. On the way home, my mistress told me he is not Greek at all, but Syrian. "That was Apollodorus, the emperor's architect himself!"

The mason beckoned to me to step out onto a giddy, windy platform at the very top of the building.

A·WICKED·TRIP

DAY XV OF SEPTEMBER

Cytheris is very proud. She has made friends with a stagehand at the theater of Pompey, who will let us into a performance there tomorrow afternoon. Our mistress will not learn of it, for she plans a visit to the temple at the same time and does not want anyone to come with her.

❀❀❀

DAY XVI

Pompey's theater is near Nero's baths, on the low ground by the big bend in the river. Inside, there is enough room for an audience of 20,000 to sit down. Not that they ever do! In all the time we were there, hardly anyone stayed in their seats. They stood up to applaud and cheer — or to shout and heckle the actors. They walked back and forth, too. Just as we arrived, half the audience left to watch a tightrope-walker in another part of the city.

The performance was unlike anything I have ever seen before. Cytheris called it a "pantomime." The star of this show stood at the center of the stage, chanting and speaking at the top of his lungs. Meanwhile, slaves made music with rattles, cymbals, drums, and gongs.

The rest of the cast acted out the story in silence. The sweeping movements they made with their arms meant that those in the farthest seats could understand the action — even if they spoke only a little Latin.

I did not like the story! The chanting star told how a woman cheated her

 husband. When some of the women in the cast took off their clothes, I covered my eyes — though most of the audience roared with laughter. One of the actors spotted us and practically lifted us from our seats, telling us, "This is no place for girls as young as you!" I was embarrased but relieved that I didn't have to watch any more.

The most extraordinary sight completed our wicked trip. As we were marched to the exit, Cytheris hissed, "Look! LOOK!"

I followed her eyes and saw our mistress sitting with some women friends in the seats above us, and she was laughing as loud as any of them. I put my finger to my lips, and we hurried home.

❀❀❀

Cytheris shouted, "We've got tickets!" (though of course we didn't), but I was embarrassed.

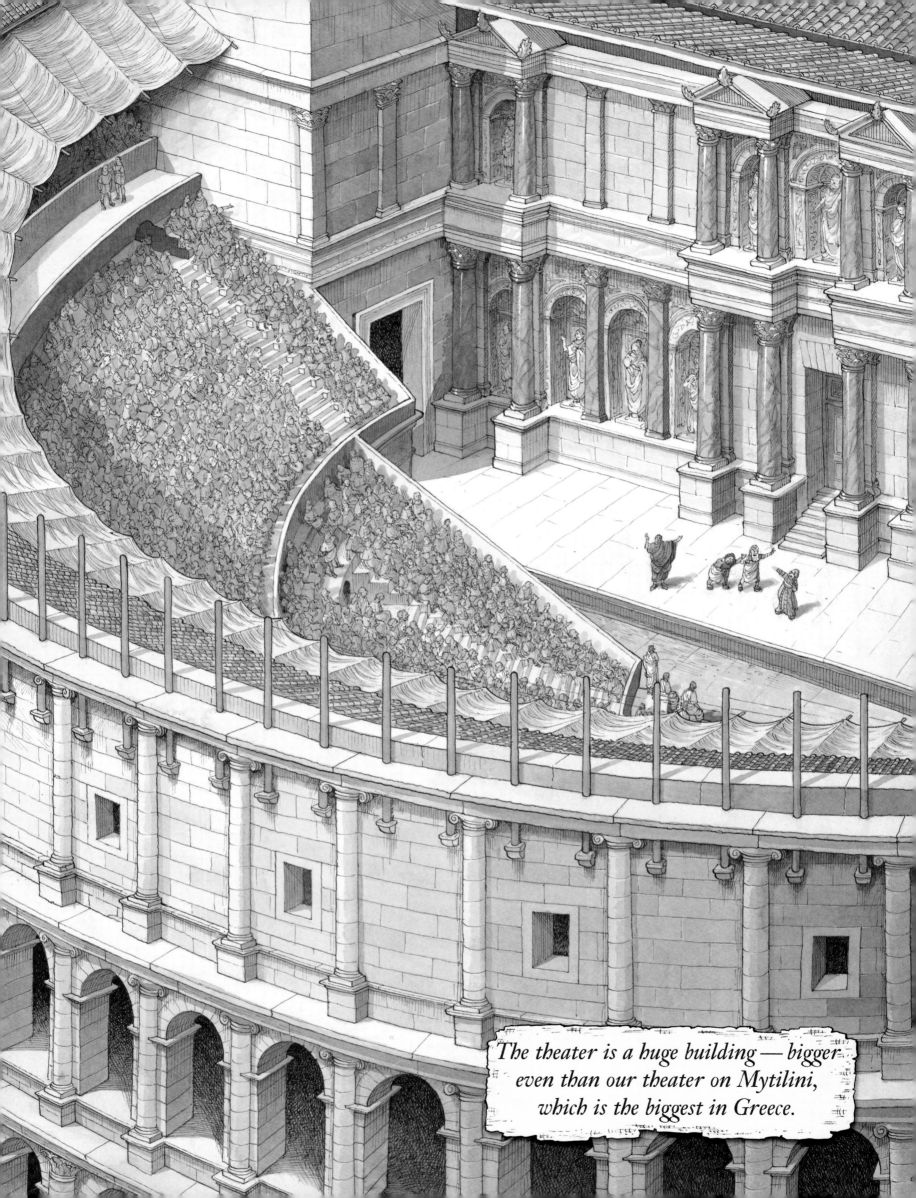

The theater is a huge building — bigger even than our theater on Mytilini, which is the biggest in Greece.

I·WATCH·A·BANQUET

DAY XX OF SEPTEMBER

Today my mistress announced that she is to hold a banquet in honor of two newly appointed senators. "Nothing too grand," she added, "just nine of us." However, I have heard much of Roman banquets, and our cook was terrified at the thought of all the work. He ran around moaning, "How will we manage in our tiny kitchen?" He was calmed only when my mistress assured him that a caterer will prepare most of the food and we will only reheat it here.

❀❀❀

DAY XXIII

I cannot quite believe the quantity of stuff that fills the kitchen and another room besides.

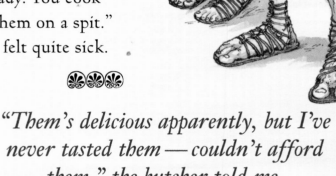

Some of it I do not even recognize. The butcher brought some beasts like rats, skinned and sewn up along the belly. I asked him what they were, and he cheerfully replied, "Them's stuffed dormice, young lady. You cook them on a spit." I felt quite sick.

❀❀❀

"Them's delicious apparently, but I've never tasted them — couldn't afford them," the butcher told me.

DAY XXIV

My task tonight is to to stand at the side of the room with a jug of perfumed water and a towel, and before guests lie down to eat, I shall wash and dry their hands and feet. I shall wash their hands between courses, too, if they command me to do so. This seems deadly dull, but I shall at least have the chance to listen to the conversation.

❀❀❀

Preparations began with the delivery of a small mountain of charcoal.

DAY XXVIII

I am so exhausted that I can hardly write, though the feast finished more than a day ago. The guests began to arrive as the sun was setting and were still here when it rose.

I have never seen such food! First there was shellfish: mountains of oysters, mussels, and spiny sea-hedgehogs. Then tiny songbirds huddled together on a golden platter. The stuffed dormice I had seen earlier arrived dipped in honey and rolled in tiny black seeds. The main courses were kid, suckling pig, and sow's udder—all stuffed and roasted.

There were entertainers, too—dancing girls who tumbled and leaped in the air, musicians from Africa, a dwarf who ate fire, and a hunchback who told jokes about everyone there.

Of course there was wine: warmed wine, wine chilled with snow from the mountaintops, wine sweetened with honey, wine flavored with costly spices. And then yet more wine, mixed with water just as people normally drink it.

Indeed, it was too much wine that ended the evening. One of the guests started talking about the new baths. He did not know how attached my master is to the project and began to rave about how "its great cost will destroy the empire."

When he finished, my master turned purple with rage. Nobody else dared to speak. Moments later he left for his room, trembling like a leaf.

The argument shook everyone, and I felt exhausted by it (and by standing on my feet all night). When I got to bed, I fell instantly asleep and awoke only when it was night once more.

"Rome's citizens already spend too much time loafing in hot water," the guest said.

I cannot remember how many desserts there were. The grandest was a vast ship at sea, made of pastry, sugar, and almonds and carrying all kinds of fruit.

A · CATASTROPHE

Our small quiet world was turned upside down yesterday. My master seemed weak and ill when he rose in the morning. When he complained of pains in his chest and numbness in his left arm, my mistress tried gently to persuade him not to attend the Senate. But he was determined to go and set off in a litter, gripping his vial of sea-grape wine.

We learned later that at the Senate House he had to be almost carried to his favorite seat. The blow came when he stood to speak: his legs would not hold him, and he fell to the ground, clutching his chest.

The senators carried him home on a tabletop, and here he lies, in a darkened room. His pulse is weak, and he speaks few words. He drinks little and eats less.

Outside the silence of his room, my mistress wrings her hands and prays at the shrine by the front door. My master's brother is here. He has used his influence to send a letter to Cratinus by the emperor's messenger. It travels at the speed of a galloping horse and will reach him in a day, for he is now stationed not far from Rome. However, even if he hastens back with all possible speed, I fear he will be too late.

✿✿✿

During the night, a physician came to examine my master. The man was a Greek, like me. He arrived with four attendants but took only my mistress into the bedchamber where my master was lying.

When they came out, he was holding my mistress's hand and reassuring her. However, as they passed a torchbearer, I glimpsed his eyes clearly and could see from their empty, hopeless look that he did not believe his own words.

An hour later, my master suffered another blow like the one that struck him yesterday. This time he did not recover. Now my master is dead.

✿✿✿

My master struck his head on the tiled floor of the Senate House.

52

Even though he was one of the best in Rome, the physician could not help my master.

DAY 1 OF THE MONTH OF OCTOBER

In the middle of the misery and mourning for my master, I have a reason to be joyful! The reading of his will has brought a fantastic and wonderful surprise.

Yesterday my master's brother fetched the will from a temple nearby where it had been stored for safekeeping. He took it into the dining room to break the seals and read the wax panels to the family.

After about half an hour, I heard Cratinus (who arrived yesterday) shouting, then he stormed out of the room in a black mood, followed by everyone else. My master's brother was the last to come out, and he called me over to sit with him in the *peristylum*. There he read to me the words that follow (for I borrowed the wax tablets and copied them):

For her bravery in saving my baby daughter from certain death in the flames of a house fire, I set free my slave Iliona immediately. I also set free her brother, Apollo, who shall

be brought from my country estate to be reunited with his sister. In addition, I give to Iliona each year the sum of one hundred denarii.

I am free at last!

"If you had shown your father more respect, he would have shown you more generosity!" my mistress shouted after Cratinus.

53

FREEDOM

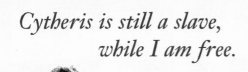

DAY III OF THE MONTH OF NOVEMBER

A month has passed since I last unrolled my diary and sharpened my quills. My life has changed so much — and yet it seems hardly to have changed at all. Apollo is with me, which makes us both very happy. My mistress sent for him several days after the will was read. He walked all the way to Rome rather than wait for a carriage to fetch him. Now he works here in the house, doing any tasks that require strength and skill — for his months on the farm have given him powerful arms and hands that learn quickly.

Now that I am free, my mistress treats me better than she did before and even says "please" and "thank you" if she remembers.

Cytheris did not speak to me for a fortnight. Thankfully, though, we are friends once more.

I am spared some of the tasks I hated most, such as emptying the piss pots in the morning, but I am still studying and looking after little Lydia.

Apollo and I have talked about returning to Greece. We could perhaps save enough from our earnings to pay the fare. However, our parents are at the bottom of the sea, and we have few relatives on Mytilini.

Cytheris is still a slave, while I am free.

Furthermore, if pirates were to attack our ship on the journey, we might swiftly find ourselves back in Rome. Then our story would start again, just as it began a year ago, with chalk on our feet and wooden signs around our necks.

No, for the present we shall stay here, for my mistress's home is now our home, and her family has become our family, too.

❀❀❀

Lydia now seems just like a baby sister to me.

ILIONA'S·WORLD

THOUGH ILIONA'S LIFE IS A STORY, it is based on historical facts. Stolen children really did work as slaves in Roman houses. Not all were Greeks: they also came from the many other countries that Rome ruled, for the Romans were the most powerful people in the ancient world. Over six glorious (and bloodthirsty) centuries, they created magnificent art, architecture, and writing. Even today we rely on Roman ideas for everything from our laws and calendar to our water supply.

·WHERE WAS ANCIENT ROME?·

Ancient Rome stood where the modern Italian capital city stands today. It was built on seven hills on the banks of the Tiber River.

The Tiber connected Rome to its port, Ostia, where the ship bringing Iliona to the city would have docked. Beyond Ostia, the lands that the Romans governed stretched from Spain (*Hispania*) in the west to Syria in the east. Rome ruled Egypt (*Aegyptus*) in the south, and the northern frontier was England's border with Scotland.

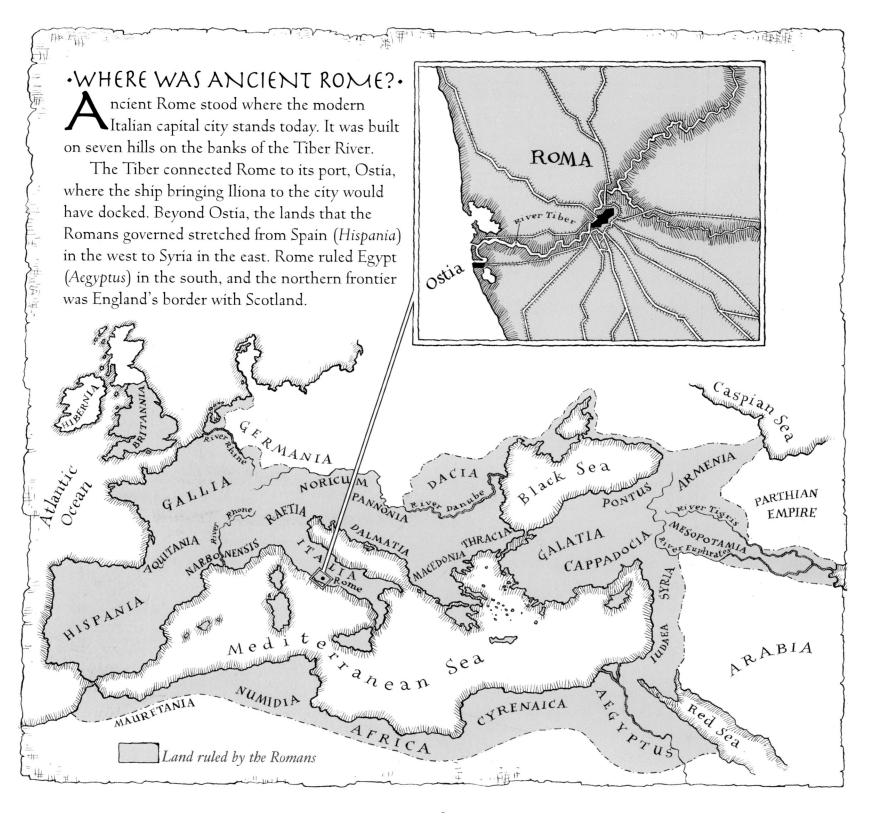

Land ruled by the Romans

ROME

·THE CITY·

In AD 107 Rome was a busy, thriving center of trade and industry. Probably three quarters of a million people lived there.

But Rome was an old city even then. People had been living in and farming the Tiber valley for more than 1500 years. According to Roman tradition, the city itself was founded in 753 BC by twin brothers, Romulus and Remus. Romulus gave his name to the city.

·THE EMPIRE·

The Empire was the main source of Rome's great wealth. Each time the Roman armies defeated a hostile nation, they were able to plunder its riches. War booty flowed back to Rome, and with it came huge numbers of prisoners who were made slaves. Furthermore, the people of the captured regions regularly paid tribute (a kind of tax) to Rome.

WHO WAS WHO?

In the second century, *emperors* governed Rome. They were not elected, as modern presidents are; they were dictators and held complete power over the people.

Emperor

Even so, the Roman people liked to believe that they governed themselves, and the emperor chose a Senate (parliament) from the city's oldest and wealthiest families. *Senators* advised the emperor but had real power only in the smaller details of running the city and empire.

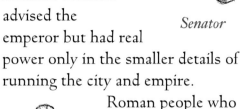

Senator

Roman people who were not members of the Senate were called the *citizens* of Rome. Though some citizens were wealthy, others were poor and owned no land. Even so, they enjoyed some of the same rights and privileges of wealthier Romans.

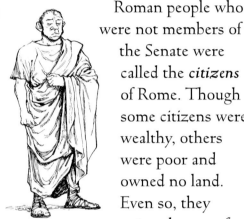

Citizen

About one twentieth of those who lived in Rome were *freedmen*. These were people who had been born as slaves but who had won or bought their freedom. Freedmen could become very wealthy, because (unlike some citizens) they could become traders.

Freedman

Slaves were at the bottom of Roman society. They were the property of their masters and could be bought and sold like furniture. The quality of their lives varied tremendously, depending on their owners. Some were beaten and starved like animals, but many lived better than the poorest citizens.

Slaves

·A SLAVE'S LIFE·

Slaves made up between one quarter and one third of the population of ancient Rome and did all the heaviest, dirtiest work.

Wealthy citizens owned astonishing numbers of them: those with farms or factories sometimes had 20,000 or more. They might have bought these laboring slaves at very low prices. However, the best slaves — the intelligent, educated, and beautiful — sold for colossal sums.

In early Rome, citizens would put their slaves to death without fear of punishment. However, by the second century, there were laws to protect slaves from the very worst treatment. Some were still beaten, but slaves could at least rely on their value as protection: only fools destroy their own valuable property.

Slavery made Rome rich, but not all Romans were happy about that: with slaves doing so much of the work, many of Rome's poor — but free — citizens were unemployed and lived on handouts of free grain and oil.

THE ARMY

I t was the Roman soldier who made Rome powerful. Fighting in enormous armies, he conquered all the territory that was to become the Roman Empire. Roman soldiers were well trained, well equipped, and not easily frightened. In a battle you'd want them fighting on your side!

·THE STRUCTURE OF THE LEGION·

A small Praetorian Guard protected Rome itself, but the main fighting forces were the Roman legions: thirty or so mini-armies trained for conquest abroad.

Legions were made up of five to six thousand foot soldiers (legionnaires), who fought in groups of eighty called **centuries**, each commanded by a centurion. An officer called the Tribunus Militum commanded **cohorts** of six centuries, and there were ten cohorts in a legion.

·SOLDIERS' EQUIPMENT·

R ome's soldiers did not just fight. They built roads and bridges too. As well as his shield and sword, a soldier carried many other useful things. Altogether his gear weighed about seventy pounds. He would be expected to march twenty miles a day with this load on his back. Soldiers had mules to carry the leather tents and the millstones they used to grind their wheat into flour.

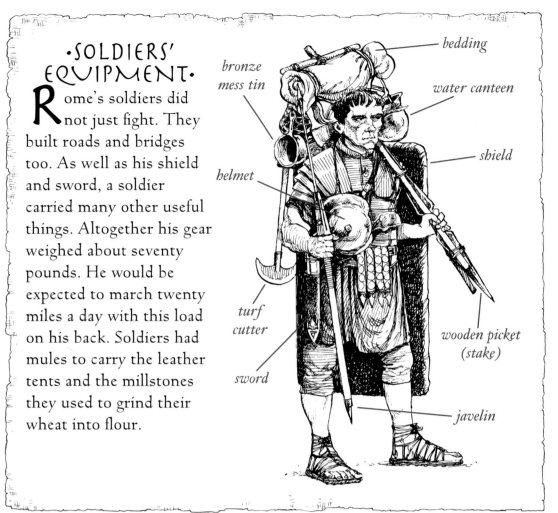

bedding
water canteen
shield
wooden picket (stake)
javelin
bronze mess tin
helmet
turf cutter
sword

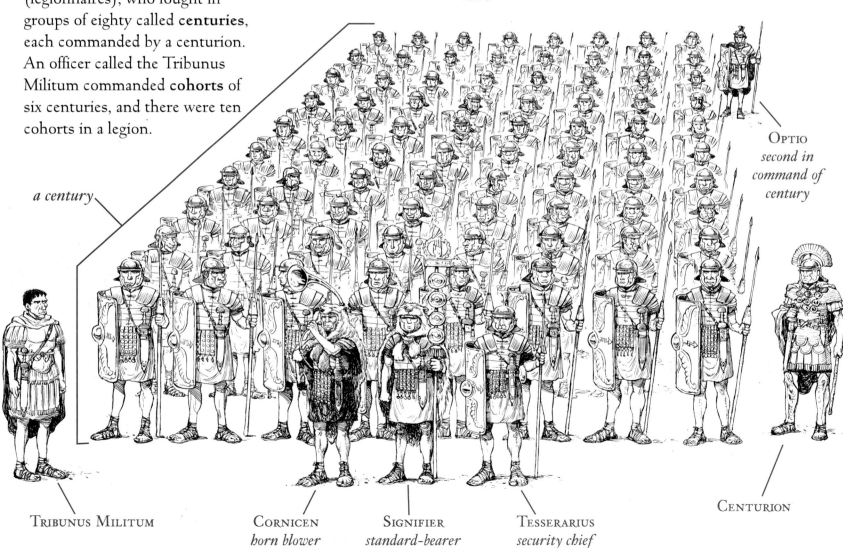

a century

TRIBUNUS MILITUM

CORNICEN
horn blower

SIGNIFIER
standard-bearer

TESSERARIUS
security chief

OPTIO
second in command of century

CENTURION

SPORTS AND GAMES

Just as we do, the Romans loved spectator sports. They were obsessed with chariot races, supporting one of the four teams — red, green, white, or blue. Slaves raced light chariots, drawn by two or four horses, around a two-thousand-foot racetrack at breathtaking speeds. It was very dangerous, but a skilled driver became a hero and could earn enough in prizes to buy his freedom.

Romans also loved to watch *munera*: battles to the death between gladiators (warrior slaves) in a specially built stadium, the Colosseum. The fights were staged by Rome's wealthiest people to show off their fortunes or to win votes in elections.

Gladiators often killed their opponents, but if the loser in a battle had fought bravely, the cheering crowd could demand that his life be spared. The winners — like chariot drivers — became celebrities.

When simple gladiator fights began to bore the audience, novelties were introduced, such as battles with animals (the fiercer, the better) or naval battles in the flooded stadium.

RELIGION

Roman people prayed to many gods. In early times they had worshipped the spirits of the natural world and of their dead ancestors. Later, they came to admire Greek religion and merged their own gods with those of Greece. The Greek god Zeus, for instance, became the Roman god Jupiter.

Rome's priests worshipped all these gods in 100 or so temples in the city, and ordinary Romans joined in festivals each year. But religion could be a private affair, too. Every house had a little shrine where people prayed to a small statue of the family spirit. There were similar statues outdoors, particularly at crossroads, where the poor and homeless prayed.

As the empire grew, so too did interest in cults (the worship of foreign gods). When Christianity spread to Rome, it seemed at first like just another cult. However, more and more Romans joined the Christian church, and by the end of the fourth century, Christianity had become Rome's official religion, replacing all others.

A charioteer driving a quadriga *— a four-horse chariot*

TECHNOLOGY

The Romans invented many things that brought lasting practical benefit to large numbers of people. We still use lots of these inventions today.

•CONCRETE•

Long before Roman times, builders bound stones together with mortar, a mixture of lime and water that became hard once it dried. But Roman engineers mixed mortar with a special kind of sand from the town of Pozzuoli, and so invented concrete. Rammed into wooden molds, concrete set as hard as rock.

•WATER SUPPLY AND SEWAGE•

As Rome grew, so too did its thirst. Public fountains on every street corner gushed with fresh, clean water. To keep the supply running, engineers built viaducts across the coutryside to carry water channels (aqueducts) from springs as far as fifty miles away.

This Roman viaduct could carry two channels of water at the same time.

Rome also had a basic sewage system. Toilets and sinks drained into pipes beneath the road outside. These emptied into the

•ROADS•

To speed the marches of Rome's legions, soldiers built roads as they went. First they surveyed the routes, planning an arrow-straight path across suitable land. Next they dug a pair of trenches to keep the road between them dry and free of mud. The road itself was built in layers like this:

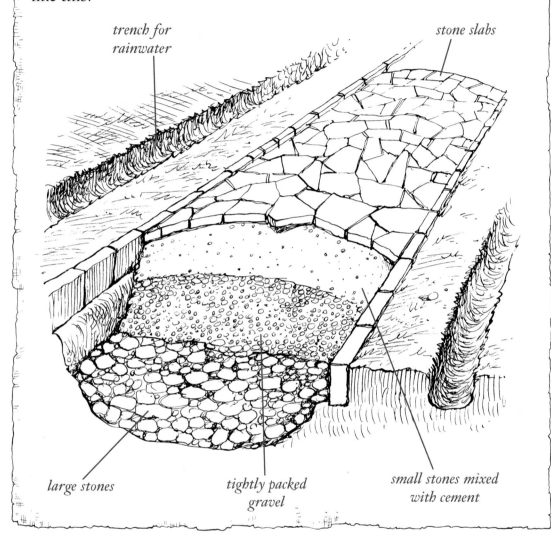

trench for rainwater

stone slabs

large stones

tightly packed gravel

small stones mixed with cement

Cloaca Maxima ("greatest sewer") and then into the River Tiber.

•CENTRAL HEATING•

Thanks to Rome's climate, houses rarely needed heating. Public bath buildings, though, needed to be warmer. They were heated by furnaces built on outside walls. Chimneys drew smoke from the furnace through channels under the floor and behind walls. Called a hypocaust, this system was like modern warm-air heating.

•OTHER ROMAN THINGS WE STILL USE•

- Books with pages are a Roman idea. Previously people wrote on long rolls of paper.
- Many of the laws that govern how we live are based on Roman laws.
- Parliaments with two "houses" follow the pattern of the Roman Republic.
- Romans measured their months by the phase of the moon, which returns to full every 28 days.

- We write with the Roman alphabet, though the letters J, U, and W were added much later.
- Many of the words that we **use** every day were **originally** in the Latin **language** that the Romans spoke. In these two **sentences** words in bold come from Latin.
- Roman masons arranged half-circles of shaped blocks to hold up wide openings in walls without cement. Arches are still used to build stone bridges and to make grand doorways and light windows.

A Roman arch

- A ring of arches creates a dome: a roof like an upturned bowl. The Romans built the first huge domes, and ever since, architects have used them to keep rooms free of supporting columns.

The dome of the Pantheon in Rome was the largest in the world for over 1700 years.

·A TIMELINE OF ROMAN HISTORY·

The story in this book is of just one year. But the period of Rome's power lasted almost 1500 years. This timeline shows some of the most significant events in that time so you can get a sense of the empire's history.

BC

753	According to legend, Romulus founds the city of Rome.
509	Romans throw out their king and start to govern themselves as a Roman Republic.
264–146	Rome fights Carthage (a rival city in what is now Tunisia) in three Punic Wars. Its victories give it control of most of the Mediterranean, including Greece and Syria.
90–82	Civil war breaks out between Rome's noble families and its citizens. A noble — Sulla — wins and rules as a dictator until 79 BC.
73–71	Seventy gladiators, led by the slave Spartacus, escape. More than 100,000 slaves join them in a revolt.
60	Two politicians, Pompey and Crassus, and a general, Julius Caesar, share power and rule Rome and its empire as a "triumvirate."
53	Crassus dies. Pompey rules while Caesar is away fighting in Gaul (France).
49	Caesar returns to Italy to challenge Pompey.
48	Caesar defeats Pompey at the Battle of Pharsalus.
45	Caesar becomes dictator of Rome.
44	Caesar's rivals murder him. They aim to make Rome a republic again.
43	A consul, Mark Antony, forms a new triumvirate with Caesar's great-nephew Octavian and Caesar's ally Lepidus.
42–32	Octavian and Antony fight rival politicians, and then each other, for power.
31	Antony, fighting with Cleopatra, queen of Egypt, is defeated at the battle of Actium.
27	Octavian, Rome's first real emperor, rules as Caesar Augustus. He brings peace, good government, and wealth to Rome.

AD

2?	Jesus of Nazareth is born in Judea (now Palestine).
14	Caesar Augustus dies and is declared a god.
29?	Jesus is executed on the orders of Judea's Roman governor, Pontius Pilate.
37–41	The cruel Emperor Caligula rules Rome.
41–54	Emperor Claudius rules. He adds Britain to the Roman Empire.
68	The much-hated Emperor Nero kills himself. In the year that follows, four different emperors rule.
79	The volcano Vesuvius erupts in the south of Italy. The towns of Pompeii and Herculaneum are buried for 17 centuries.
98	Trajan becomes emperor. His conquests in Dacia (in southeastern Europe), Nabatia (Jordan), and Parthia (Iran) extend the empire to its maximum size.
115	Jewish people in Egypt, Libya, Cyprus, and Judea rebel against Roman rule.
235–284	Twenty-five different emperors rule Rome. Chaos engulfs the empire, and northern tribes threaten its borders.
285	Emperor Diocletian splits the empire into eastern and western halves to make it easier to govern.
324–337	Emperor Constantine "the Great" reunites the empire and rules from Byzantium (now Istanbul, Turkey). He makes Christianity the official religion.
337	Constantine dies, and his sons divide the empire among themselves.
410	German tribes reach the city of Rome and raid it for the first time.
476	The German general Odoacer forces Rome's last emperor out and makes himself king of Italy. The Roman Empire falls.

GLOSSARY·AND·INDEX

Page numbers that are <u>underlined</u> show where unusual words that Romans would have used have already been explained. Other unusual words are explained here. Words shown in *italics* have their own entries, with more information or pages to look up.

G

GALLEY 5 A long, low ship with sails and oars.

GAMES 40–43, 59 See also *munera*

GAUL 38, 61 A *province* of the *Roman Empire*, situated where France is today.

GLADIATORS 40–41, 59

GODS 23, 59

GOSSIP 36

GREEK 5, 8, 9, 11, 18, 19, 22, 29, 33, 34, 44–45, 52, 56, 59

H

HECKLE 46 To shout abuse.

HORSES 23, 31, 59

HYPOCAUST 60

I

IUNIUS 18, 20, 22, 26 The *Latin* name for June.

IULIUS 28, 30, 32, 34 The *Latin* name for July.

J

JAVELIN 58 A long, light spear used as a weapon.

JULIUS CAESAR 61 A powerful politician, general and, later, *dictator*.

JUPITER 59

JUPITER (TONANS) 30

L

LABORERS 34 Farmworkers.

LATIN 8–9, 11, 15, 19, 33, 46, 61 The language of Rome.

LAUREL WREATH 23–24

LAWS 26, 56, 58, 60

LEGION 58, 60

LEGIONNAIRE 18, 58

LETTERS 6, 34

LIME 45 A white powder produced by burning limestone.

LITTER 14, 52 Seat mounted on two poles, upon which a master could be carried around by his slaves. See also *sedan chair*

LOT 9 Goods sold together at *auction*.

M

MAIUS 12, 14, 18 The *Latin* name for May.

MAMILLARES 14 Cloths to tie around the chest.

MAMME 29

MANUMISSION 15, 18

MARBLE 20, 27, 39, 44

MARINERS 6 Sailors.

MASON 44–45, 61 See also *stonemason*

MORTAR 60

MULES 30, 58 See also *donkeys*

MUNERA 40, 59 See also *games*

MYTILINI 5, 13, 15, 20, 28, 30, 33, 47, 54

N

NERO'S BATHS 14, 44, 46 See also *Agrippa's baths* and *baths*

NET MAN 40, 42–43

NICHE 26 A space set into the wall where small objects are kept.

O

OFFERING 30 A gift to the *gods*.

OIL 8, 14–15, 38

OLIVES 8, 31, 34, 35

OMEN 30 Something people believe gives a clue to what will happen in the future.

ORNATRIX 39 A hairdresser.

OSTIA 8, 56

OVERSEER 4, 9–11, 15, 35 Someone who supervised workers on behalf of their master. See also *bailiff*

OX 13

P

PACE 19 A distance equivalent to the length of a stride.

PANTOMIME 46

PAPYRUS 5, 6

PEDAGOGUS 12 A tutor.

PERISTYLUM 20, 36, 53 A covered courtyard surrounding a small garden.

PHYSICIAN 52–53 A doctor.

PIRATES 6–7, 54

PLUNDER 57 To steal, usually using force.

POMPEY 46, 61 A military leader and ally of *Julius Caesar*.

POSTMAN 31

POZZOLANA 45

PRAETORIAN GUARD 58

PRIEST 30

PROVINCES 38 The lands that were part of the *Roman Empire*.

PURSUER 40–41, 43

Q

QUADRANS, QUADRANTES 14, 19

QUILLS 5, 54 Pens made from feathers, sharpened at their tips.

R

RAM 7 A long, armored point extending underwater from the front of a ship that was "rammed" into enemy ships.

RAEDA, RAEDAE 30–31 A covered wagon.

REMUS 57

SOURCES

Writers and illustrators owe a debt of gratitude to the authors and artists whose works inspire them. Richard Platt and David Parkins are especially grateful because they searched in more than seventy books for details that would make the text and pictures of Roman Diary authentic. There isn't room here to list them all, but the following are among the more recently published books.

Adkins, Lesley & Roy A.: **Dictionary of Roman Religion**

Beacham, Richard C.: **Spectacle Entertainments of Early Imperial Rome**

Bennett, Julian: **Trajan, Optimus Princeps**

Biesty, Stephen: **Stephen Biesty's Ancient World: Egypt, Greece, Rome in Spectacular Cross-Section**

Bradley, Keith: **Slavery and Society at Rome**

Carcopino, Jérôme: **Daily Life in Ancient Rome**

Connolly, Peter, and Dodge, Hazel: **The Ancient City: Life in Classical Athens & Rome**

Casson, Lionel: **Everyday Life in Ancient Rome**

James, Simon: **Ancient Rome**

Langley, Andrew, and de Souza, Philip: **Roman News**

Marks, Anthony, and Tingay, Graham: **Romans**

Paoli, Ugo Enrico: **Rome: Its People, Life and Customs**

Richardson, Lawrence: **A New Topographical Dictionary of Ancient Rome**

Robinson, O. F.: **Ancient Rome: City Planning and Administration**

Roman Numerals

Numerals 1 to 12

I	II	III	IV	V	VI
1	2	3	4	5	6

VII	VIII	IX	X	XI	XII
7	8	9	10	11	12

Roman Numeral Symbols

I	V	X	L
1	5	10	50

C	D	M
100	500	1000